FOREIGN BODIES

By the same author

Snakes & Girls
(New Poets Award, University of Leeds School of English Press,1970)

In All the Spaces On All the Lines
(Phoenix Pamphlet Poets Press,1971)

FOREIGN BODIES

Christopher Pilling

FLAMBARD

Acknowledgements

Acknowledgements are due to the editors of the following publications in which many of these poems have appeared: *Adam's Dream: Poems from Cumbria & Lakeland* (Charlotte Mason College, Ambleside,1981); *Ambit, New Poetry 1, 2, 9* (Hutchinson with the Arts Council, 1975, 1976, 1983); *Between Comets: for Norman Nicholson at 70* (Taxvs Press,1984); *Cellar Press; Critical Quarterly; Four Poetry & Audience Poets* (Leeds University,1971); *Iron; Lancaster Festival Anthologies* (1983, 1984, 1986, 1990, 1992); *London Magazine; New Christian Poetry* (Collins Flame, l990); *New Hope International; The New Lake Poets* (Bloodaxe Books, l991); *The New Statesman;The New Welsh Review; Northern Poetry Two* (Littlewood Press, l991); *The Observer;The Oxford Book of Christmas Poems* (Oxford University Press,1983); *Pennine Platform; Platform; Poems for Christmas* (A Peterloo Anthology,1981); *Poetry Survey* (Poets' Yearbook, 1977); *Reynard; Sceptre Press; Solstice; Speak to the Hills* (Aberdeen University Press,1985); *The Spectator; Starwheel Press; Tracks; The Times Literary Supplement; Vision On* (V.E.R. Poets' Anthologies); *Voices of Cumbria* (Westmorland Gazette, Kendal,1987); *Workshop New Poetry*. Some of the poems have been broadcast on BBC Radio 3 *Poetry Now*, Radio Leeds and Radio Nottingham.

The charcoal and graphite drawing reproduced on the front cover is *Flail* by Geoffrey Morten.

Flambard wishes to thank Northern Arts for its financial support.

Published in 1992 by Flambard Press
4 Mitchell Avenue, Jesmond, Newcastle upon Tyne NE2 3LA

A CIP catalogue record for this book is available from the British Library.

ISBN 1 873226 03 9

Typeset by Writers Inc, Newcastle upon Tyne
Cover design by Peter Morrill
Printed in Great Britain by Athenaeum Press, Newcastle upon Tyne

for Sylvia

and all embracing foreign bodies

He, that would not be a stranger to the universe, an alien to felicity, and a foreiner to himself (T.B. 1586) ... *mintinge to goon in to foreine derknesses* (Geoffrey Chaucer c.1374) ... *rose out of his amazement ... foreignly beholding himself* (George Meredith 1880). *Part of the electric matter natural to the body must be repelled, to make room for the foreign electricity* (Joseph Priestley 1770) ... *a Forreign Spirit, stronger & more eager than the Spirit of the Body* (Francis Bacon 1626).

This is the name that chaceth away the clips
Of foreyn dirknesse (John Lydgate c.1430).

When a being or object reveals itself to feeling, it, so to speak, loses any vestige of foreignness or estrangement (John Caird 1880). *Car JE est un autre ...* (Arthur Rimbaud 1871) ***FUN*** *to* ***HUG*** (British Encyclopedia Vol.5)

The lemons, the brandy, the sugar & the nutmeg were all foreigners (Joseph Addison 1716).

Contents

Walking the wall

Sentences after Hell Fire Corner

The snapped fern stalks are trip wires.
The buried branch I hacked was a human arm.
Slicing a beetroot I stop short of the thumb.

She tells the ears of the fern not to trip.
Reeds cluster; grasses twist intricately.
Add vinegar, a bitter wine.

We walk the wall, gingerly, with momentum.
You can live for 20 minutes with a bullet in your head.
Sand for sandpits not sandbags, Krzysztof.

Lichen patterns underfoot, grey lichen shapes.
Rats rhyme with cats, swell on blood, going blind.
Warsaw will kiss in a sewer.

The shrapnel rain stings our cheeks.
On the map *Stink Post* is designated *Odour Houses.*
Trousers need peeling from the knees.

Periscopes along the parados and Very lights.
Waterlogged shell holes a quagmire where heads protrude.
Baked apples with raisins through the centre.

We raise our heads to see wind scud the reservoir.
The canal water is sluggish as if weighted with blood.
Branches and saplings are blown across the sweet-pea trench.

The field

I stopped in the open under an apple bough,
with no tent but the dark, no pillow

but stooks — my Gallic itinerary crossed
by nightfall. I took my rest,

seeing stars between leaves. Sleep was slow
to come. A wind blew at the bole

of the tree, soughing. Leaves
replied. The stack came to life.

Mice tickled the straw with their patter:
the straw's teeth chittered.

Branched phantoms shook my head.
The sky, charcoal with cloud,

smouldered within. I slept.
My sleeping bag lay across France, wrapped

me from harm, the dawn journey to Ypres.
A light rain on my face woke me.

War photographer from the age of 14

Don McCullin in Vietnam

"The green parrots flew to another perch.
The sniper had picked off another of
our men who'd only moved his head an inch
from the ground." Another shot. The parrots fly
in an arc every time. They come to rest
near the photographer who's waiting poised.
There is no sign from the God the wounded
call to. Only green parrots moving through
the air. The photographer'd been angry
with God when his father died. "I used to
comb his hair... I hate the noise the shutter
makes as I'm pressing it. It's like shooting
a man a second time. I can hear the
sniper kill my father every year."

Count down
after Vietnam

Talking to oneself is the first sign...
I'll phone: lift the receiver; 5, 4, 3, 2,
index in turn in four adjacent holes...

Laces device devices... intra-uterine?
A distinct recurrent purring. Do you
imagine her in wedges, in Scholls

or lace-ups...? A handsome nude of leg
before the skirt or the great divide
of dressing gown and no time to button

as she takes to the stairs... *Shakespeg*
packed MSS in his hold-all, re-allied
against the Vietcong (Sir, General Dutton,

attackanddestroy, if you say so,
if you're responsible, say *your* finger's
on the trigger). My finger juddered

but one more turn — instep out — means no
more purring, no more flingers
on of dressing gowns. The mouthpiece shuddered...

Misdeeds etc

Joking of the world's misdeeds etcetera
he leaned to his friend and wrenched her hair.

The onions burning in the frying pan
were domestic comestibles not symbols for man.

When the knife had sliced through the
rings she had wept: smarting microcosms.

The gestures of morning were as random
as uncombed strands after nightmare.

She'd sidestepped the bull, gained the fence
which gave. He was over with time to spare.

Bull, onions were as much a part of her
as head of hair, tears, presentiment of war.

Table

The green damask cloth, shaken
of crumbs, is relaid
over all the table edges.

It's those knives & forks
that keep on insisting
the table be turned

into a battlefield. A reluctant
spoon has no hold over them.
They slice & spike on.

Tomato, onion, cucumber
are contained till the knife
& fork set to.

Their motions are functional.
To see them as a dance
against death is far-fetched

like the added salt
and the wood under
the green damask tablecloth.

Art of travel, 1855

Do take a coffee service when you camp,
advises Galton. Wear flannel against
your skin. If your muscles are not too tensed,
thanks to carpet slippers, you'll not get cramp.
Blücher boots are vital — for if you stamp
your landing foot on river sand condensed
enough to squeeze a sting-ray out that's sensed
you're there for the stinging, you will not tramp
much further. Then blackwater fever may
delay your party in the bush. Fish hooks,
knives and beads handed to the village chief
before the trek may make the natives stay
with you if you're panicking. Tell the cooks:
Coffee from a china cup's a great relief.

Brainstorms

I *Gogol to Danilevsky*

I'm going to shave off all my hair so as to relieve my aching head. I'd like a wig when I get to where you are — Montmartre is it? — all red curls perhaps, or dark brown and parted down the middle — or I shall freeze without! *Thoughts* can then get started once more *like a swarm of disturbed bees* and my imagination can take wing higher than Saint Peter's Church. Folly that: *I can neither live nor write.* I'll wring its fat neck — puffed Melancholy!

Still *the lines come out limply.* I should sing.

Mama's had me invent the brolly!

II *Annenkov to Gogol*

I think, Nikolai Vassilyevich

If you leave your manuscript that you've worked on in a trance,
oblivious of billiard balls clicking in the saloon,
of the multi-lingual chatter, of each waiter's glance
as he passes the small table you've had brought
in specially, oblivious of the smoke, of the spoon
rattled in a glass as a thirsty afterthought
by a tipsy traveller on his way from France
to Liguria, as he'd confide to anyone —
if you leave your manuscript that they've looked at askance
— you are the oddity, the one who seems to shun
the real things in life: the banter, the tang and tart
flavour of the local Albano wine — and chance
to suggest to me a stroll down to the heart
of the Gardens of Sallust, not for romance
nor to escape the fug of the inn, but to retain
the ambience of the *poem* created by your thirst,

8

if you leave your manuscript that's ceased to advance
and, taking your umbrella in case of rain,
turn a corner by the Barberini Palace, prance,
twirling your umbrella until it flies off, and burst
into Ukrainian folk-song, you'll never stop your dance.

III   *Gogol to Father Mattvei*

I have already heard voices, as I told Dr Over.
I must atone, you say they say, for the sin of writing
Dead Souls, by entering a monastery; I shall die
unblessed if my second volume comes as a second slur.
What is it all for? I ask you. And you prophesy
I shall have to pray two days before an icon.

I'll refuse all food but spoonfuls of pickled cabbage;
I'll burn the dreadful manuscript before I am purged.
Imozemtsev will prescribe an aperient and water —
laurel water, that is. I shall present an image
of extreme consumption to Tarasenkov. The shorter
my life, the fewer bones of contention will stick in my gorge.

Evenius will recommend force-feeding; Alfonsky
I be mesmerised; Sokologorsky assumes
that musk is the answer, but the letting of my blood
will prove the most popular — Klimenkov will agree
to the point where, instead of two leeches, he will stud
my nose with six. I can already smell the fumes

of the mustard plasters they'll apply. I'll have to drink
calomel in bed at night and suffer Spanish fly
on my nape, ice on my head. Was it all a waste of ink?

Globe artichoke,

survivor from Roman times, *Cynara Scolymus*,
if you prefer...
I trust you're not one of those who deem us
too fiddly or full of fur?
Have a lemon handy — foil
air when you slice off my nether
regions (or I'd go black as oil).
Pull off my leather-
y outer scales before you boil...

Archecokk, hartechooke — that's how
your English man-
about-town used to speak of us, but now
that it's common or garden *choke*, we're an
ordinary sort of thistle
for perfect herbaceous borders. Your Italian,
though, will eat our babies raw (or sizzle
them in the frying pan),
with *vino bianco* to wet his whistle.

Pietro Aretino to Titian on his *Annunciation*
Venice, 9 November 1537

The dazzle of Paradise. Angels on
a shimmering of clouds. Hear the wing-beat
of the Holy Spirit that's left the Seat
on High as a dove. A rainbow has shone
over a landscape at dawn that's brighter
in its refulgence than an earthly fleet-
ing one seen after rain. A shade whiter
than snow, the lily held by Gabriel is where
it's caught by radiance coming from within.
And yet he's modest — his eyes do not dare
ruffle her peace, her divinity. Say
milk and blood were mixed to tremble as skin.
A saffron robe hiding nakedness, sin
takes fond leave of your paint and mouths *Ave*.

Pietro Aretino to Madonna Maddalena Bartolini
Venice, 10 December 1537

Two jars of olives — what a red letter
day for me! My deepest thanks. They were dressed
as only you know how, have passed the test
of *bons viveurs* already, whose better?
The Spanish flaunt their size; the Bolognese
(not grafted either — in a sense suppressed)
keep the bitterness they draw from the trees.
Yours are succulence itself; nutritious
too — dare I ask for more — no man forgives
parsimony!
        So, your son's delicious
wife has filled out and yes, you must be pleased —
long legs, full lips, full breasts — my sedatives! —
buttocks as round and plump as your olives,
all the tastier, I dare say, when squeezed.

Mrs Hall confesses

from Mrs Hall's diary, 1853

Mr Hall had his pocket
picked in the Forum today.
"This harmonises morally
with the physical decay
around us: loss of lira,"
he reflected, "loss of aura."
I could not feel enough either way.

And I cannot appreciate why
Cardinal Newman came
here many times in spirit.
"Scenes of ancient heathen fame,"
were what his heart yearned toward
— and yet he was "wedded to the Lord."
Mr Hall told me he felt the same.

He's a clergyman too.
He climbed St Peter's dome
right into the golden ball
("It has no apertures"), a tome
of Cicero in his pocket.
He said it was "intensely hot."
I'd rather be back at the *Inghilterra* (or home).

I'm sometimes disgusted at my indifference to Rome.

In Florentine circles

So the road out to Florence from Pisa
has leaning plane trees on either side!

Raphaël really knew his *Mona Lisa*
in Maddalena Doni, said the Pitti guide.

Why's Bartolomeo Bimbi numbered figs
like our hotel room, my passport, your visa?

The quattrocento water-trough with sprigs
of hosepipe from †*Aprile's* geyser

has vied for our attention with whose fine
Annunciation? Martini's or da Vinci's?

Whose *Madonna and Child* has added meaning
with pomegranates, saints or finches?

What work of art in Florence, what design
by Brunelleschi, has left us leaning

closer together by several inches?

† *Aprile*: our hotel in Florence

Venice triptych

I *Before going into St Mark's out of the rain*

I took Sylvia to see the Doge, first
in the Ducal Palace: he wasn't there.
Rain spouted from the roof and slapped the bare
buttocks of the courtyard. With our eyes pursed,
we tried, in his absence, to pierce the gloom. Thirst
for one painter's vision lured us to stare
beyond the visual at Europa's share
of the bull's affection. Veronese burst
out in breast flesh and a cow looking on
lowed in complicity. "He's in the square,"
she called from a bull's-eye, "there's a pigeon
on his wrist pecking crumbs." But he was gone
when we got down. "You're seeing things! Swear
you won't be raped by that bull, religion!"

II *Bellini's **Virgin**, Santa Maria dei Frari*

It's the angels that worry me, playing
their instruments inaudibly until
the concierge closes the church. "You will
have to come back after lunch." So saying,
he locks and shuffles off. "Leave them praying,
all the saints." All concierges shuffle
and all saints pray. We do up our duffel
coats against the October wind. Weighing
the pros and cons of *trattoria* fare
we temporise, buy stuffed olives, fresh rare
thin slices of meat and a length of bread. Soon
we're eating and downing wine in honour
of one who's waiting for us, Madonna
of the sacristy, keeping the angels in tune.

III *Out in the Lagoon*

"There are five of us, leaning together
and held round the nape — also the torso —
by metal stays. Backs braced to the weather
we stand, our knees wet and our feet more so!
Now if one of us loses his footing
we take the strain. If your falling brother
leans on you bodily, you're off putting
the world to rights. We're helping each other
and the world passes us by in its boats:
steamers, gondolas with outboard motors,
Noah's Ark — in fact, anything that floats.
We are not five of your floating voters!
Persuasive waves browbeat our reflections.
We're gathering moss, and there's no defections."

On our toes

"Shall we be friends, not stand on tiptoes?"

Merry dithyramb

Red
raw
girl
said:
"Curl
up
and
cup
your
hand
to
my
heart;
blue
high
art!"

Sunday morning rondel

She plays the piano in her dressing gown
leaving me in the attic to sleep.
The communion wine will have to keep
and mature. Just say we're out of town.

Red fillet of lamb is sizzling down
below, where, splayed by an octave leap,
she plays the piano in her dressing gown
leaving me in the attic to sleep.

Her clothes hang on without a frown
— unlike cassocks in a furrowed heap
after matins. Having roasted our sheep
we stay attuned. With a snatch of *John Brown*
she plays the piano in her dressing gown
leaving me in the attic to sleep.

Being out in the wet

If whenever the rain is falling
steadily you can feel it too,
let us experience each other
readily, not as wet through,
but as feeling the raindrops
falling on each other's skin,
refreshing it completely, not
walling us with wetness within.
(Indoors our preoccupations clothe.)
Such sensuality's conditional
then on your coming out in the wet,
touch sensing each irrational
otherness: with open pores you
quiver at the tickle of each drop
that fleshes us so tinglingly we
shiver lest the rainfall stop.

Kitchen rack

A frieze of knickers, footloose socks,
shirts with ungovernable arms,
those jeans the children wanted washed
again, one nightdress. Had I qualms
about her love.... My mother swashed
sheets in the dolly tub. Now clocks
reiterate: the rack's still there
and these clothes hang on, no soapier
than they ought to be. Here's my wife
in knockabout garb, cornucopia
in briefs, socks that've come to life,
and a turban — she's washed her hair.
Now, fluffing it out — she's no Sikh
though I'm a votary... (You can reek
of *Domestos* more than once a week!)
— she has me in a trance, giving it
auburn lights. And shiny, is dancing
for me, solo... *Sole mio...*
Up on the rack, the knickers flit,
the jeans, with a patch enhancing
their appearance, flap *con brio*.

The only hope

Quick to jump to conclusions, quick
to take things to heart, quick
to see faults in herself and sick
in the knowledge of the hurt she thinks she's done.

I neglected my children
for hours at a time.
I lost my temper all too readily
and said unforgivable things.
I was not at home for their coming home from school.

This knowledge brought
the sickness, this knowledge taught
her nothing to stem the sickness, this knowledge wrought
a sea-change in her body. Then no tide turned.

Tell her she left the children
only an hour or two a day;
tell her if tempers fray
there's no harm in exploding;
tell her a mother needs a life beyond the home.

And she says she knows these things,
but she says she *feels* some things
deep down, she stings
her flesh with a rash of them, scratches the spots until they burn.

The fire of self-reproach takes over,
it burns away mere reason,
it eats her with its flames,
it leaves her charred and black and empty.
She's lost the feeling in her tongue.

Time they say's the healer,
but paralysis is stubborn, a dealer
of a death-in-life blow, a wheeler
of hallucinations, a flail that's dizzied her and she's succumbed.

And the only hope for healing is the children.

Laburnum

One pistil
two green & downy
three dark brown

twist

five black grains
— sixes & sevens —
(all good children

stick)

One poison
not too well implanted
three golden

rain

She lies silent...

She lies silent, her head in *The Plague*,
on the verge of sleep (verge is hardly the word
for this losing of consciousness, this vague
running of words before the eyes, a blurred
horde of rats on their final legs, muffled
squeaks in the far reaches of the mind
where there is no verge). She is unruffled
by the tumours that solidify the rind
of silence, knowing deep within that she can lose
herself in reading or in sleep or in both at once
and the sanatorium of her marriage will use
her kindly, will tend each ugly protuberance
with a doctor's skill, with a nurse's oversight,
and, as a panacea, will put out the light.

Roundly

The world is everything which is the case
In your eyes what makes the living reel
Is roundly the what of our embrace

The electric room where we face to face
The lightning which shocks us to reveal
The world is everything which is the case

No thunderclaps are heard for us to trace
The voyage of a storm we cannot feel
Is roundly the what of our embrace

One forked flash (no boom) is out of place
But fuses us within a pausing wheel
The world is everything which is the case
Is roundly the what of our embrace

In the outhouse

The swallows leave as I arrIve.
They hear my tread, dive
out through where there is no door.
What was it I came for?
The nest is packed mud, trim
with feathers. FInger over the rim
singles three eggs. Tentatively
I raise one high enough to see
its shape and colour — bone
wIth *terracotta* specks. Beamgrown,
this nest is for a family:
three, two, one, then an empti-
ness, an empty hole...
Oh yes, I was out to fetch coal.

Light leaves

The light is on in the room.
The curtains are not drawn.
The light's replica gilds the leaves
of tea-roses bedded in the lawn.

The grass grows apace and the leaves
shine. Still, the rose flower,
shock pink and scented by day,
is lustreless. Where is the mower?

He sees the leaves rise and
fall but does not feel the breeze.
He sees the light outside
and trembles in his darknesses.

Belladonna

She's gone to the garden for chives,
scissors akimbo;
she's Atropos, one of my wives,
the slim limbo
dancer, the it's all done on salads one
who's taken to growing
all the vitamins we'll need in the garden
she's constantly sowing...

She's back, and I'm out there pissing
in the lean-to bog,
my flies agape, the urine hissing...
Now a trog-
lodyte would have heard her passing his cave
in his nightshade swoon
for she comes working her scissors like a rav-
ing worshipper of the Hewn!

I feel for my genitals: if
she comes too close
she'll have them for sweetbread, stiff
or comatose —
They'll go well with salad, you can hear
her thinking, hot *or* cold.
That's how I feel, hot *and* cold! I sweat with fear.
— If I may make so bold...

A wife's assumption

"Why should the one
whose ideas on sex are more antiquated than the mastodon
play up to men?

The ten commandments
are what she holds to but she wittingly sends
shivers down implements.

Do you really mean
Thou shalt not commit adultery is an open invitation
to take the mastodon

by the nippled teeth
and suck for all you are worth
— its jaws being extinct you'd not be fearing mastication —

shalt not allowing
you might, and might well, if the urge were strong,
the forbidding fruit there for the plucking?"

"Your free and easy
moral assumes we should be sexier with an all-consuming reason.
You, like her, are queasy."

Caution against caution

Beware *anorexia*
nervosa in your bid to be sexier.
Slim's a prison,
a euphemism for thin, bedizen
an apology for woman how you may.

Be rounder, eating
a little of what's a treat in
store if you don't discount a
cache beneath the counter
of the health food display.

A little of what you
can't admit to fancying will do
for me to fancy you.
Fat, fat, fat, you mutter throwing caution to
the winds which blow you my way.

Door at loggerheads with chrysanthemums

Door

Looks uninspiring, or so you think,
but whoever opens and closes
me must see that I'm not just poses
like you and always needing a drink.

Chrysanths

Can you admit, though, without a twinge
of conscience, that since your mind dozes,
you're just functional? Some noses
even prefer our scent to roses...
A drop of oil almost makes you cringe!
You'll let anyone push you away...

Door

I'll admit that you should have your say...
But why must you stay open all day,
slaves to the public, always on view...

— And with that — and the wind — he slammed to.

An affair with a chalr

Why the wooden chair begIns
walking towards me on its
four stilted legs
I shall never guess

Why tiny breezes blow
from its woodworm holes
each like a miniature slipstream
I shall never know

Why its bentwood back
leans forward to embrace
could-it-be-me I would love
to discover

And why it stumbles
just before it reaches
where I am sitting on its upright
sister I still need

to explain to my satisfaction

Fran

Her name is in the books I've bought at Oxfam.
There's an illustrated *Guide to Amsterdam*;
I, Jan Cremer, denizen of City Smut;
A Play of St George by a Poet Laureate;
a Narayan novel, published in Mysore,
bought in New Delhi, October '84:
The Vendor of Sweets; *Headhunters*, a pamphlet signed
by the poet, Keswick, 1979 —
quite an odd collection. And I picked them out
almost as if my hand were guided — no doubt
I am a kindred spirit, but amassing
things that she's grown out of — only past passing
fancies. What possessed her to give them away?
I squeeze them in my shelves — Fran is here to stay.

After *Illuminations*
Rimbaud on the run

You abandoned writing, your dreams no longer cohered,
were not common enough, not forthright women.
You set sail wordlessly to your *douceurs*...
from barred holds heard the voice of volcanoes,
of arctic grottoes melting. The guns you ran
at Harar were bad business, a bad business.
What one will do with a lack of tangibles!
You voyaged to discover erotic landscapes,
erect Orients and equally infrangible Floridas:
deserts sear lusts, however loose-limbed your contortions;
only pyramids of stone and an unamused sphinx
lay their bellies to Egypt: flat juxtaposing.
The highest tower's windows have cracked, its orifices
filled with sand, which could not run out.

Tristan's ghost, sea-dog

My yellow loves are now at large
Anaemic embarkations had me by the short hairs
Shingles for you with yr francs sewn in your breeches
Mine a posthumous circulation

Armless gull   have you seen your mirror
I nailed a dry toad on a cross of mantelpiece
Not a squeeze of fluid in its flat relic
Outside   the sea against Roscoff harbour

Webbing on ox-floors   Knots   Clay pinions
My father's a shipping magnate at Morlaix
And you make your catches   my Roscoff fishers
You swill the residue out by the scuppers

Blood and salt for my yellow loves
My small creased yellow toad
You are resurrected on the slapping mainsail's mast
For me [†]*an Ankou* and all that comes with the sea

[†]*an Ankou*: Corbière's nickname, meaning Death

33

Cast away

from an anonymous journal — discovered on the Island of Ascension by a Captain Mawson of the ship Compton — relating the author's being set on shore there by order of the commodore and captains of the Dutch fleet, for a most enormous crime he had been guilty of, and the extreme and unparalleled hardships, sufferings and misery he endured from the time of his being left there — the 5th of May, 1725 — to that of his death.

I Useless to relate how I've strained my eyes —
   often, misled by a distant sighting,
   an earnest want of delivery will rise
   in my shipshaped mind's eye, highlighting
   my frenzy. The ceaseless wild ocean boom
   intermixed with the sun's quite searing rays
   presents to my senses a yellow gloom
   like the moon when part obscured. When it stays
   I expect to see in every streak and cloud
   what I take to be a propitious sail...
   Then dreadful the shock! And my cry out loud
   as before my gaze the thing can fail
   to materialise. What I see — no longer there —
   has left within me the depths of despair.

II The spring I found after weeks of searching
   has run dry. I drink the blood of turtles.
   I read my prayerbook constantly. Lurching
   into recrimination, thought hurtles
   off down unmade rock-strewn tracks. Voices drum
   on my brain with every side-step. It's: "You...
   bugger! bugger!" hits hardest. Satan's come
   for me — he's at my tent-flap with his crew,
   banks on my dying of thirst. I must drink
   my urine now. If only water would gush
   from the rock as it did for Moses; ink
   of the squid would be a godsend — and lush
   green purslane meadows. That hullabaloo,
   those shrieks, must be boobies to the rescue?

III   Having lived on birds' eggs,
birds shot with a fowling-
piece, onions and rice,
I must bestir my legs
daily, the sun scowling
at me, for my true vice
is unforgivable,
I must find water and
the wherewithal to subsist.
If I'm thought liveable
I'll cross the burning sand,
my body will resist
hunger, thirst, but even
so, as a skeleton...

IV   Lust
for
man
has
sentenced
me
here.

Fear —
raw,
intense
as
can
be...

Ophelia

was Elizabeth Siddal in a bath
under which oil lamps were kept burning.

Millais, absorbed in the folds
of her dress, did not see her turning

blue with cold. The lamps went out
unnoticed. Elizabeth froze.

Millais' gaze had been transfixed:
the bath was the stream,

the heat of his passion for the folds
Ophelia's madness,

both mixed, mixed, mixed as *idée fixe,*
unrequited until the hots and colds

of paint were one with Elizabeth
who, like Ophelia, was close to death.

The lid

Clanging the lid of the stainless steel teapot
she contained the rising steam
of what it is like to be on your own
in a silent house with a husband cremated.

Foreign bodies in the escritoire

My mother's been dead over twenty years.
Rummaging, as I have been, through a box
of my father's writing equipment: rocks
of sealing wax, ink concentrate, ears
of mould on a nutcracker — Look! Here's
a threepenny bit but only two locks
to go with seventeen keys! — it shocks
me to alter the past, have latent fears
unearthed: However much I may treasure
a young, resilient, beautiful, caring
mother concerned to write a weekly letter
to her parents, I cannot get her measure
and the discovery of her false teeth glaring
among rusty paper-clips makes things no better.

The clown

executes
tricks, *volte-face*

to amuse
the populace

who all have
the naïve

assumption
that the plum

cheeks, the black
lined sacs

for the eyelids,
the flour head,

the laid-on lips,
the *pomme* nose

are false
and ridiculous.

Feeling one's a little different

Feeling the ache of
is it wings burgeoning,
his shoulder blades
shrug to ease the matter.

If it should be wings
the circles he could move
in would be considerably
reduced.

Even folding pinions
into cars or armchairs
would be a tribulation,
practice making perfect.

The arch comments,
the sidelong lances
would be a devil of a malediction.
And what's not said.

One's overt leanings
would make one out
an outsider. One would be
one. Also a nonentity

on trying to fly.

The jugglers

On this reach the stones are opaque.

Reassurance has arch feet,
hands in pockets
of mist,

toecaps pebbles.

Arp   Brancusi   Moore
held clear stone against their palm:
hands saw.

Bell & navels, egg, mother & child.

I crouch,
take handfuls of shingle,
throw into thin air,

catch catch reflections.

A good day's fishing

The old man, he must be nearly
ninety, is standing in his garden
with, of all things, a fishing rod
and he's casting it, the early
bird, to catch whatever is lurking
in the lobelia bed, an odd
centipede or a worm? Are there
really fish swimming round the flowers
that only he knows about? Gherkin
trout no hotelier would recognise?
He reels in his line, turns to where
our fence divides us. In the hours
that pass his muscles will not harden
for he casts again among the fireflies
— hovering above our compost heap —
with an easy turn of the wrist, a wily
savoir faire, flexing like fish that leap.

You, standing in a landscape

                                        Bonfires
are formidable sights. We do not ask
what they burn.
                       The smoke obscures
the deft hill curves above *The Waltzing*
                                Weasel,
       but only partially,
                    momentarily.

            A small flock of silent black birds
       has no ulterior motive perched in an
               angular tree.

                         Lines of snow bank
the west of fields. A late sun cannot
dissuade them.

                 Water rumples, flexes,
flashes,
       leaps,
           tumbles,
              tends, crimples
the satin of itself,
           adjusts its tacking.

You stand in this landscape alert to its pressures,
take on its elements,
           swim in its fluency,
                 are it,
and your enigmatic self.

Stones lie...

Stones lie inert, of course.
They turn in profligate rain

so slightly.
You observe their smoothness, their edges

but do not see their moving.
They take their time —

quartz time: flint time, time of bloodstone,
time for landscapes to settle,

as though they were immobile,
as though their stones lay unmoved,

aglow with rain, glowing
with the spendthrift rain...

You'd call them inscrutable — you haven't changed!
Unchanging, they gleam like stones,

not turning an eye.

Spring-cleaning

She's been out putting the fellside to rights:
those rocks were askew, that sheep-track too rough;
a dust for those hollows with feathers a chough
should never have shed. Adjusting her sights

to a waterfall she has altered its course
and the stones when dry she has smoothed and stacks
in the air's airing cupboard — where the slope lacks
the cover of heather, or rowan, or gorse.

The wind is too wayward and often too wild!
The hail no respecter of tender skins!
The sun will do till grass yellows and thins!
She's stopped wind and hail; the weather's re-styled

so the hills can sport split skirt and beanie.
Scabs of lichen have been treated with salve.
Valley cows are transfixed, each teat has a valve.
Barbed wire has gone: sheep's wool's soft and sheeny

until the rains. Rain's all right — it washes
and even the mountains need to be cleaned.
The ferns have their heads raised, the swamps must be preened.
She has been out in cagoule and galoshes

but not to go for a strenuous climb
for its own sake. She's been on a mission:
now the fellside must be above suspicion;
the rivulets had better be running on time.

Time for change

The clock face hardly changes;
its hands are not meant to touch —
they swivel from a centre, their ranges
only so far, never too much.

Minutes step with an even gait,
clockwork even, always just
catching up. There's a spate
of ticks to tell before the rust.

They set the pace and we must follow
suit. Their tricks are crotchets
that voice each catch. Swallow
your axis and try out duets.

Not so much apart

Time, the receiver,
watches us go bankrupt
and swoops down

scattering our last assets
at the instigation
of one Monsignor Death

whose malignant growth
has brought me
to this hospice and my knees...

Going through my pockets,
Time (Time again!)
lives in hope of finding pence

— which he will look after
or place as penny lids
on my glazed eyes

when my pounds of flesh
can no longer
look after themselves...

Calling Death Monsignor
I must see him as a foreign body
like my cancer

but it's so much a part of me
I realise as I fight it
and him and go down

cursing his rule of thumb.

J.C. in a prospect of beasts & flowers

Here's my John Clare; after all you've got your hawk!
You're all hovering and claws: I'm going mad.
Did I write a sonnet and assume the talk
of a rose would betoken love? I stalk
game in the ditches of Helpston. It's bad,
the doctors say, to stoop with such sudden speed
on the unsuspecting vole. I am sad
if you catch adders and I renounce my creed
for I believe in the God of snakes; hear him walk
down the hedgerows I peered into as a lad
when love was any nesting place and plumped bead
of hawthorn. Nurses call my ragged robin rose.
I raise myself on an elbow, for I am freed
from J.C. and for your hawk I'll trade my crows.

In his shoes

Do you mind, she asks,
handing me a suicide's shoes.
Try them on:
they're the same size as you take.
A present from the jumble sale.

The rims hold firm;
there's been little wear in these.
As I tauten, secure
the black laces there is give at the wrists.
I stand and walk.

Peter for example

I   Even the disciples took to their heels:
Men who could leave their nets and their tax
Collecting to tread in your steps, to wheel

In the stripes of your grace. Through cracks
In the armour of light, they could feel
The inching of the night you were alone

And the cross. That his raw bare hands could fail
To bring in the nets and were chafed to the bone
And brought in the nets — such was the weight

Of the catch for Peter — and that in the court
He could disown his master, not extort
The rent of love. He raced to the gate

Of the tomb to check the women's fancy talk.
Before the wind rose over the waves he could walk.

II   Before the wind rose over the waves he could walk
To the apparition who strode towards them, bound
For the boat, determined to follow, caulk

Of faith in his sandals. Peter was not sound
Of mind with a ghost in the wake: he would
Take his courage in both feet and astound

Himself by a miracle if this were no blood
Brother. Down with the risk of being drowned.
Phantoms that talk! Anyone can walk on the sea.

A pathetic fallacy to account for his sinking!
He knew Jesus. Jesus took over his thinking.
The Holy Spirit is a saving mystery.

And having crossed over they came to Gennesaret.
When the men of that place knew him he was well met.

III   When the men of that place knew him he was well met
By the brands that flicked in the High Priest's yard.
The temple police and elders had played their card

Well, trumped the Galileans. The High Priest's valet
Had lost an ear — that was the extent of the debit.
Judas had owned his Rabbi but had reverted

With a kiss. All the other disciples had deserted
After Jesus' words: "Do you take me for a bandit
That you come with swords and cudgels for my arrest?"

Peter returned to the net where he sensed he belonged
And his salt tears after the cockcrow attest
That he was a willing catch who distantly longed

To be grilled by the flames of a house's distrust.
In the first floor room an unsettling of dust.

Prayer

is a wise conundrum.
We can't stand up to it;

it takes us by both hands,
knowing the responses.

We can't trust ourselves
to such links

and foolish postures
against space.

> We can't bring ourselves to
> ourselves out there.
>
> Our clothes lie prostrate
> outside a warm bed.
>
> Anything we might petition
> is at several removes.
>
> We stay put
> with our bodily intentions.

The piano lesson

after Matisse: The Piano Lesson (1916-17)

You sit at the piano, reluctant
to play all those heartless black notes...
Already your right eye has clouded over
— Could any cloud have the shape of a metronome? —

One side of your head is paralysed
but your weather eye is open for the least hint
of what your mother must be bearing for you, her son
— *I was almost naked for his birth, I'm naked now for how he plays* —

Behind your head the teacher's chair
has grown taller and the teacher's summery dress
has assumed the severity of a nun's habit
— On her perch she's angular as the bar lines on the stave —

Outside there's the park and its uncut grass
reaching up to the open window with all its blades
— Not one is sharp until it strikes
a green note in the music room

and your left hemisphere is sparked into being.
Suddenly the piano keys start to glow,
your fingers pick out the blades of grass from the score

and your mother, brown as the earth, has her hand between her legs
         with pride.

a miró

blob   said the head

for woman

and moon

blob

the dog's nose

full stop

take it from me red
sun spot the dog

breast the woman black
hole imploding

plop

3.031: *La belle captive*

after Magritte: La Belle Captive (1947)

*"It used to be said that God could create anything except what would be contrary to the laws of logic. — The truth is that we could not **say** what an 'illogical' world would be like."*
Wittgenstein: Tractatus Logico-Philosophicus, 3.031

The words are moving   away from things.
Ceci n'est pas une pipe, wrote Magritte
on his painting of a pipe. His dove sings

in the ribcage. Not a note. His street
at night — the house lights are on — is a day-
time scene. The words are moving away:

they carry the world   of a meaning
with them. The pipe I suck is a briar;
it is not a pipe, though my lips are on fire.
The dove in the ribcage is preening

and can't possibly sing... Overweening
this early Wittgenstein or I'm a liar!
Eve: *"Put the colour of my desire
to your lips — is it russet or greening?"*

Stanza

after Matisse: Girl with a black cat (1910)

Marguerite M. holds a black cat she could be tweaking.
The black cat doesn't sing like Teresa Berganza
but it has the shape of her lovely phrasing. Panzer
divisions are blacker — metaphorically speaking.
This sinister moggy, though, leaves us with a sneaking
suspicion that he's the devil: Mario Lanza
about to hit top C. A red-breasted merganser
drake's dark green head looks black because the shrieking
of a feline drives him far downstream where his colours
are dulled by distance. I'll end this extravaganza
with: The creature that's rarin' to kill is as dull as
ditch water near to. Marguerite's not in organza
but her best dress can still be torn by the annuller's
claws. Which, by the look on her face, 'd be a bonanza.

Picasso's eye
or The dictates of art

after Picasso: Le Gobeur d'Oursins (1946)

To swallow sea-urchins
you need to bare your feet and turn them inwards so that one bulbous little toe touches the big one of the other foot;
you must put on a sailor's horizontally blue and white striped vest and lower your head so that your neck above (or rather below) your vest is the shape of a chef's hat perched on your hair-lines;
you should roll up your bell-bottoms to just below the knee so that one retains the shape of a small bell or candle-snuffer;
you need to file off the longer fingers of your right hand; grow whiskers at the edges (but not above) your blubber lips — yes, they'll have to be blubbery;
your left thumb and lower arm must resemble a seal poised with a knife handle at the underside of its neck;
you must align the knife blade with the crease of your right trouser leg and pick up a sea-urchin from the sitting room carpet — Watch the prickles miss your instep —
you need to place the urchin you're intent on swallowing plumb centre below your nostrils and off-white lemon eyes and blow off all the spikes.

The actual swallowing is a simple matter, but not even Picasso can give you that. Several of his *sailors* have already swallowed sea-urchins, but of course you don't see it happen. His *Pêcheur assis à la casquette* is actually swallowing a lemon though.

Lemon

The answer is Eureka
if you squeeze them dry.

Hills above Villafranca
melt from the eye.

Tamarisk

My trunk aspires to basking in the roads
for you, for me, for your salt lips;
there all constructions will be codes:
drowned cities, handsome sea-glutted ships.

Tamarind

Kukkuripada's tree has the body's cleft.
The thought of awakening and the semen
are the tamarind. When they are eaten
by the crocodile, how many seeds are left?

Ginkgo

The Maidenhair, I've heard, is a holy tree
grown in a Chinese garden. Two-lobed
fans cool my trunk. You kneel
before you enter the temple, lightly robed.

Nude in 21 states

after Matisse: Pink Nude (1935)

I invited you to be my nude.
I cut you out in coloured paper
many times. "I'm your paper-shaper,"
I'd say, "changing your shape," quite imbued
with your fickleness. "Oh! they're plain crude,
those bulges, those... limbs! Do I taper
off the edge? You're cutting a caper
in pink which hardly reflects my mood!"
"Quand les moyens se sont affinés,
que leur pouvoir d'expression s'épuise,
il faut revenir... aux beaux bleus, aux
beaux rouges, aux beaux jaunes." That's what I'd say,
and go on snipping while you just freeze
into sensuous flat shapes that glow.

Andrée's bloom & the anemones

Her skin took the light as no
other model's had.
The light couldn't resist her
red hair — flecks
of gold-bronze at her crutch and scalp.

Flies, flicked off in thought, stuck.
His fingers, inept at anything,
pincered a brush
for her rotundities.
A circle should never be round.

The curves hold.
Tenacious pain grappled for the roots
of the last anemones. He was
their fresh freedom
to blossom as only they knew how.

A winged camel is sighted over a Quaker Meeting House near Sedbergh

i.m. Basil Bunting 1900-1985

A string of camels was pulled into the sky
by a crow mistaking the drover's headdress
for a cheese. Did the camels' humps turn to wings?
The drover is lost without his turban — why,
he cannot get the gist of anything unless
his head is protected: the sun really stings.
Not long ago at the caravanserai
he'd replenished the camels' water supply.

Basil Bunting told this story of the cheese
at a Literary Society Dinner
and I can hear him champing at what camels
have as a bit. His humps, or rather hunches,
keep him going and he won't get any thinner
as he sails over Briggflatts now. Nothing trammels
his flight. Like his fledged ubiquitous *spuggies*:
†*Night, float us. Offshore wind, shout* his epiphanies!

†from the Coda of *Briggflatts*

Black earth is fertile, wild silk still is

Should I catalogue the deeds of Hoang Ti and sense I am writing a Canto
         LIII...
Hoang Ti usurped the power of the Prince of Cereals Chin Nong
assuming a Name that befit a Chinese Emperor became the Yellow Ruler
         in 2698 ante Christum
taming 272 tigers as military beasts, inventing bricks, making money from
         precious stones, gold & copper
his novel organ twelve bamboo lengths three pipes for each of his wives
         the longest
for Si-ling-chi her silk-worm industry gave employment to many hands.
Bird tracks inspired Hoang Ti to create the radicals
all 540 radicals for the Shuo-Wen, a *vade mecum* of exoteric signs...

The Cantino peters out at this point unless each of the 25 males
sired by Hoang Ti be allowed to take history forward
unless the bird tracks no longer single signifiers on white snow are
         advancing
unless the sounds of organ pipes reach the ears of Shun,
Yao his ideogram eminent, Chun his ideogram wise, Yu his ideogram
         reptile,
Shun knew that music should draw out the son whose verb is I sing.

Good Friday:

for Mozart's Requiem Mass in a Munich church
the small orchestra and choir are out of sight.
They were practising into the previous night
so everything would be perfect — none would lurch
off into alien notes, as if a fickle
Philistine were joining in the psalmodies
in cold blood. — They're anathema, foreign bodies,
when they mar the purity of a canticle.
One of the choristers had praised the composer
for concentrating her mind so well that now
she sings without a care in the world, pure tones
and joy in sustaining the Lachrymosa.
One of the orchestra will go home to Dachau
with his violin. I feel music in my bones.

The meeting place

after Rubens: The Adoration of the Magi (1634)

It was the arrival of the kings
that caught us unawares;
we'd looked in on the woman in the barn,
curiosity you could call it,
something to do on a cold winter's night;
we'd wished her well —
that was the best we could do, she was in pain,
and the next thing we knew
she was lying on the straw
— the little there was of it —
and there was this baby in her arms.

It was, as I say, the kings
that caught us unawares...
Women have babies every other day,
not that we are there —
let's call it a common occurrence though,
giving birth. But kings
appearing in a stable with a
"Is this the place?" and kneeling,
each with his gift held out towards the child!

They didn't even notice us.
Their robes trailed on the floor,
rich, lined robes that money couldn't buy.
What must this child be
to bring kings from distant lands
with costly incense and gold?
What could a tiny baby make of that?

And what are we to make of
was it angels falling through the air,
entwined and falling as if from the rafters
to where the gaze of the kings met the child's
— assuming the child could see?

What would the mother do with the gifts?
What would become of the child?
And we'll never admit there are angels

or that somewhere between
one man's eyes and another's
is a holy place, a space where a king could be
at one with a naked child,
at one with an astonished soldier.